j   Van Dyke, Henry
3-4   The Other wise man; retold by
         Pamela Kennedy

The Other Wise Man

Kennedy, Pamela, 1946—
        The other wise man / by Henry Van Dyke ; retold by Pamela Kennedy
; illustrated by Robert Barrett.
        p.   cm.
        Summary: Journeying with the other Magi to Bethlehem to see the
newborn Jesus, a fourth Wise Man delays to help others in need but
eventually finds his King.
        ISBN 0-8249-8396-3
        1. Jesus Christ—Nativity—Juvenile fiction. 2. Magi—Juvenile
fiction. 3. Christmas stories. [1. Jesus Christ—Nativity-
-Fiction. 2. Magi—Fiction. 3. Christmas—Fiction.] I. Barrett,
Robert, 1949- 1ll. II. Van Dyke, Henry, 1852-1933. Other wise
man. III. Title.
PZ7.K38490t 1989   89-7590
[Fic]—dc19   CIP
                                                                 AC

Published by Ideals Publishing Corporation
Nelson Place at Elm Hill Pike
Nashville, Tennessee 37214

Printed and bound in the United States of America.

ISBN 0-8249-8396-3

The illustrations in this book are rendered in oil on board
and using live models.
The text type was set in Garamond Light Roman.
The display type was set in Abbott Oldstyle.
Color separations were made by Rayson Films of Waukesha, Wisconsin.
Composed by The Font Shop, Nashville, Tennessee.
Printed and bound by W.A. Krueger, Olathe, Kansas.

The Other Wise Man

Henry van Dyke

Retold by Pamela Kennedy
Illustrated by Robert Barrett

IDEALS CHILDREN'S BOOKS

I n the days when Augustus Caesar was the ruler of
many kings—including Herod, who reigned in Jerusalem—there lived among the mountains of Persia a
certain man named Artaban.

Artaban was one of the Magi, men who study the
heavens in search of truth about God. He and three of
his friends from far away had made a wonderful discovery.
In the ancient writings they had found a promise that at
a special time a beautiful new star would rise in the eastern
sky. At the rising of that perfect star, a great King would
be born. He would be the Truth sent from the One God—
the Son of the Most High.

Artaban believed the time was very near. He had sold
his house and all he owned to buy three jewels to carry
as gifts for the newborn King.

Now as the sun began to set, Artaban reached into his colorful silk tunic and brought out the three great gems: a sapphire as blue as the Persian sky at night, a ruby as red as the first rays of sunrise, and a pearl as white and pure as the snow on a mountaintop at twilight. Artaban held the priceless gems together in his hands and gazed into the darkening sky.

That was when he first saw the tiny spark on the horizon. He watched it grow larger and larger as it rose higher into the sky. Flashes of light surrounded the newborn star, gleaming with red and blue and purest white.

"It is the sign," exclaimed Artaban. "The King is coming and I will go to meet him!"

Artaban's three friends had said they would wait for him only ten days after sighting the star. He knew he must race to meet them at the Temple of Babylon, or they would leave to seek the King without him.

Quickly saddling Vasda, his fastest horse, Artaban galloped off, barely stopping for food or drink. He rode across brown mountain slopes and level green plains. He passed fields of nodding poppies and orchards of peaches and figs. He picked his way carefully over rocky mountain passes and crossed swirling rivers.

Poor Vasda was exhausted and could hardly walk as night fell on the tenth day. But Artaban knew it was still three hours' journey to the meeting place and urged his horse onward.

Suddenly, Vasda stopped as if afraid, and Artaban saw something in the road. He slid from his horse and approached the dark shape for a closer look. It was the body of a man. Artaban felt the man's forehead and listened for the sounds of breathing. The man seemed dead, but as Artaban turned to go, the poor man groaned, reached out one hand, and grasped the hem of the wise man's robe. The man was still alive!

But Artaban saw that without help the sick man would not live through the night. If Artaban nursed him, the man would recover quickly. But Artaban would be too late to meet his friends at the Temple. Artaban turned his eyes toward the star he had been following and prayed, "God of Truth and Light, show me the way of wisdom, which only you know."

Then he turned back to the sick man. Lifting the man gently, Artaban carried him to the foot of a palm tree. There he gave the poor fellow sips of cool water; and mixing a healing potion from the remedies he always carried, Artaban poured this too between the man's dry lips. For several hours Artaban cared for the man as he slowly regained strength. Finally the man awoke fully and asked, "Who are you?" Artaban told the man of his quest.

"I have nothing to repay you for your kindness," said the man as he prepared to continue his journey, "but I will tell you this. From our Hebrew prophets we have learned that the Messiah will be born in Bethlehem, not in Jerusalem, and that is where you must seek him."

Hurriedly thanking the man, Artaban dashed to his horse and galloped off toward the Temple. Although Vasda fled over the ground like a gazelle, the sun's first rays were shining as they entered the Temple grounds. Anxiously Artaban searched for his friends, but they were gone. Under a piece of brick he found a note which read: "We have waited past midnight and can delay no longer. We go to find the King. Follow us across the desert."

Artaban sat upon the ground and covered his head in despair. "How can I cross the desert," he cried, "with no food and an exhausted horse? I must return, sell my sapphire, and buy a camel and food for the journey. Only God knows whether I will lose my chance to find the King because I stopped to show kindness."

And so it was that the other wise man sold his precious sapphire, bought a camel and supplies, and set out across the desolate desert. By day the sun burned with terrible heat and at night the chill winds pulled at his flowing robes.

After many long weeks, Artaban arrived in Bethlehem. Searching through the town, he came upon a stone cottage. Sitting inside was a young woman rocking her baby to sleep. Artaban knocked at the open door, and the woman motioned for him to enter. Seating himself on a low bench, Artaban told the woman of his three friends and the baby for whom he searched.

The young mother listened, then nodded, saying, "Yes, there were three strangers from the East who came and gave precious gifts to Joseph and Mary and their newborn son. But the strangers left suddenly, and just last night Joseph took his little family and disappeared. It is whispered that they have fled to Egypt to escape some unknown danger."

Artaban's heart sank. He had failed once more. Seeing his despair, the woman placed her baby in a small cradle and rose to prepare a meal for the other wise man.

Suddenly, there came the noise of wild confusion and uproar in the street. Women screamed, men cried out, and the clanging of swords and armor filled the air. Artaban ran to the doorway of the cottage as the woman snatched up her baby and hid in the shadows of the room.

"The soldiers! The soldiers of Herod are coming for our children!" The shouts filled the air as a towering centurion approached the tiny cottage. Artaban stood still, filling the doorway, and glared into the soldier's eyes. Then he slowly reached into his tunic and brought out the huge ruby, watching the soldier's face gleam with greed.

"I am all alone here," said Artaban, "and I am waiting to give this gem to the centurion who will leave me in peace."

Quickly the soldier snatched the jewel; then he turned and shouted to his men, "March on! There is no child here."

The soldiers ran on down the street, leaving the other wise man and the grateful mother weak with relief.

"O God of Truth, forgive me for telling this lie and for giving to a man that gift which was to be for you. Will I ever be worthy enough to see the face of the King?"

But the woman in the shadows spoke softly over her sleeping child. "Because you have saved the life of my little one, may the Lord bless you and keep you all your days."

The next morning Artaban decided to follow the baby King and his family into the land of Egypt. So he left the town of Bethlehem and traveled on. But his task was not an easy one.

Month after month, year after year, the other wise man searched for his King. He traveled to the pyramids and to the Sphinx, to the palaces of the Pharaoh and to the River Nile. But always the answer was the same: no King was to be found.

Although he did not find anyone to worship, he found many to help. He fed the hungry and bought clothes for the naked. He cared for the sick and visited those in prison. Still he carried the beautiful pearl close to his heart, hoping one day to present it to the one he continued to seek.

After thirty-three years of searching, Artaban had grown very old and tired. But he decided to take one last journey. He thought that perhaps he might find the clue that would at last lead him to the King.

Arriving in the city of Jerusalem, Artaban watched a shouting, pushing crowd work its way through the narrow streets.

"What is this uproar?" he asked a shopkeeper.

"Have you not heard?" the man replied. "Two famous robbers are to be crucified today along with another man called Jesus, who claimed to be the Son of God. He is going to be executed because he said he was King of the Jews."

Artaban's heart raced at the man's words. Could it be that he had found his King at last? Perhaps if he hurried, he could arrive in time to offer his great pearl to the enemies of the King and rescue him before he died!

Gathering his robes around him, Artaban hurried up the dusty street. Just before he reached the city gates, he was stopped by a troop of soldiers dragging a young girl. The girl was crying, and her hair and dress were tangled and torn.

Seeing Artaban, she cried out, "Have pity, kind sir! My father died owing these men a great sum of money. I am to be sold as a slave to pay the debt. Please save me from a life worse than death!"

Artaban had missed his King twice before as he helped someone in trouble. He was so close to the end of his search—could he give it all up now? Then he looked into the eyes of the helpless girl. One thing was certain—rescuing her would be a true deed of love. And wasn't the ability to love the gift of the One True God?

Artaban took the pearl and placed it in the hand of the weeping girl. "This is your ransom, child," he said. "It is the last of my treasures which were to be given to the King."

At that moment, the sky darkened and echoing peals of thunder rumbled through the hot streets of Jerusalem. The walls of the houses rocked to and fro as the earth rolled as the waves of the sea.

The soldiers fled in terror, leaving Artaban and the girl alone.

Suddenly, a heavy section of roof tile broke loose and crashed down upon the other wise man. As Artaban fell to the ground, he heard a quiet, yet insistent, voice speak to him over the thunder.

"Artaban," the voice called softly, "you have been a good and faithful servant. I was hungry and you fed me. I was naked and you brought me clothes. I was in prison and you visited me. Come now to the rest I have prepared for you."

"Not so, Lord," whispered Artaban with the last of his strength. "When did I do all these things for you?"

And the voice answered, "Whenever you helped one of my people in need, you helped me."

The peace of understanding fell upon Artaban's soul like a gentle rain and he smiled. His journey on earth was ended. His treasures were accepted. The other wise man had found the King.